Amazons and Their Men

by

Jordan Harrison

SAMUEL FRENCH

FOUNDED 1830

NEW YORK HOLLYWOOD LONDON TORONTO

SAMUELFRENCH.COM

ISBN 978-0-573-66246-1   Printed in U.S.A.   #3751

IMPORTANT BILLING AND CREDIT REQUIREMENTS

All producers of *AMAZONS AND THEIR MEN must* give credit to the Author of the Play in all programs distributed in connection with performances of the Play, and in all instances in which the title of the Play appears for the purposes of advertising, publicizing or otherwise exploiting the Play and/or a production. The name of the Author *must* appear on a separate line on which no other name appears, immediately following the title and *must* appear in size of type not less than fifty percent of the size of the title type.

In addition the following credit *must* be given in all programs and publicity information distributed in association with this piece:

Workshopped by Clubbed Thumb as part of Summerworks 2007
and by The Playwrights' Center as part of PlayLabs 2006.
First produced by Clubbed Thumb at the Ohio Theatre in
New York City, January 2008.

AMAZONS AND THEIR MEN premiered on January 5th, 2008 at the Ohio Theatre in New York City. The Production was Directed by Ken Rus Schmoll, with Sets & Projections by Sue Rees, Costumes by Kirche Leigh Zeile, Lights by Garin Marschall, Sound by Leah Gelpe, Props by Alan Edwards, the Composer was Matt Carlson, the Stage Manager was Jeff Meyers, Assistant Stage Manager Courtney James, Costume Assistant Marielle Duke, Wig Stylist Jessica Gaffney, with the following cast:

THE FRAU.....................................Rebecca Wisocky

THE MAN .... Brian Sgambati

THE EXTRA...................................... Heidi Schreck

THE BOY...Gio Perez

CHARACTERS

THE FRAU (35-45)
on camera, she plays **PENTHESILEA,** queen of the Amazons.

THE EXTRA (30s)
on camera, she plays several different nameless **AMAZONS.**

THE MAN (35-40)
on camera, he plays **ACHILLES.**
off camera, he plays **THE MINISTER OF PROPAGANDA** and **MUMMY.**

THE BOY (20)
on camera, he plays **PATROCLUS** and, later, **THE GODDESS OF LOVE.**

HISTORICAL NOTE

This much is true: In 1939, the German film director Leni Riefenstahl started work on a film version of Heinrich von Kleist's *Penthesilea*. Riefenstahl herself was to play the starring role. When Germany invaded Poland, filming was abandoned and Riefenstahl's screenplay was lost. All that survives are production notes in which she delineated the 34 key scenes of the film. While I was inspired by these facts, this is not a historical or biographical play: Riefenstahl isn't named; even the war isn't named. Historical details are meant to sneak through, as if by accident, at the end of a take.

PRODUCTION NOTES

This play takes place *On Camera* and *Off Camera*.

In the *On Camera* scenes, we should feel the narcotic pull of a camera's view, but there must never be an actual camera on stage. An important question, of course, is: How much of the action do we actually see? It seems to me that some kind of physical shorthand is desirable, so that the actors aren't doing exactly what they're describing. (It is probably unnecessary to pantomime drawing an arrow in a bow, but the actors might follow the path of the arrow with their eyes.) Above all, the staging of the On Camera scenes should help us to "film" the scenes in our heads, complete with pans, zooms, and jump cuts. In the Clubbed Thumb production, we used a wheeled platform in many scenes to help create these filmic illusions. When the actors were wheeled closer to the audience, it had the look of zooming in for a close-up; when the actors revolved, it looked as if the "camera" of our eyes was circling around them. Please note that scenes ending with the stage direction "End of fragment" require a more jagged edge – in the Clubbed Thumb production, these scenes ended with the sound of a reverberant editing splice.

On Camera scenes begin with titles, like so:

THE GREEKS DECIDE TO OFFER THE AMAZONS AN ALLIANCE. PENTHESILEA REFUSES.

These titles – some of which are taken from the scene headings of Riefenstahl's treatment – are projected at the beginning of the scene.

Off Camera scenes feel like a return to earth; a return to logic; a return to chairs and inside voices. But, aside from a couple noted exceptions, the characters still wear the classical costumes from the Frau's film.

NOTES ON THE FILM ACTING

When we watch films from the '30s and '40s with contemporary eyes, the performances often seem to flirt with the ridiculous. It's not that film acting was bad – it was just unabashedly emotional and grandly gestural in a way that we seldom see any more. There was a crispness of movement, particularly in period films, as though the actors were moving on rails. This is the kind of acting that is required in the On Camera scenes. I suggest watching Anne Baxter in *The Ten Commandments*, Olivia de Havilland in *Gone with the Wind*, Garbo in *Camille* – and of course Leni Riefenstahl's own performances in *The Blue Light* and *Tiefland*. Although the On Camera scenes in AMAZONS have elements of camp, the actors aren't camping it up – they're giving great performances in a time when the standards of greatness were very different.

EPIGRAPHS

If there is room in your theater's program, it would be good to include the following quotes:

"Nazi cinema exploited the limitations of human imagination, seeking to obliterate first-person consciousness and to replace it with a universal third person."
> – Eric Rentschler, *The Ministry of Illusion*

"In Penthesilea I found my own individuality as in no other character."
> – Leni Riefenstahl

On Camera.

PROLOGUE

THE FRAU. *(voice only)* Interior. Night.

(Light on **PENTHESILEA,** *blonde and beautiful.)*

THE FRAU AS PENTHESILEA. The camera first sees her reflected in a lion's eye.

(Light on **ACHILLES,** *in chains.)*

THE MAN AS ACHILLES. What kind of woman keeps lions for pets?

PENTHESILEA. A woman who loves fresh kill.

ACHILLES. What is your will with me, woman?
If you wanted me for meat, we wouldn't be having this conversation.

PENTHESILEA. But instead of answering him, she waves her hand...

(Light on the **EXTRA,** *who fans them with a palm frond.)*

THE EXTRA. ...And a hundred golden ladies summon a desert breeze.

ACHILLES. An army of women!

PENTHESILEA. In Amazonia, the male is a rare flower indeed.
Now, brave warrior, relax. Cool your brow in the court of Penthesilea.

ACHILLES. Why have you put me in chains?

PENTHESILEA. She doesn't need to answer –
Her close-up says everything.

THE EXTRA. The music plays. The focus softens.
Penthesilea falls in love with Achilles.

PENTHESILEA. *(smoldering)* Let me be food for your ravenous dogs.

Let me be breakfast.

Let me be dust.

THE EXTRA. Achilles falls in love with Penthesilea.

THE MAN AS ACHILLES. *(smoldering)* Let me trail like a corpse behind your flashing-hooved horses.

Let me be baggage.

Let me be ballast.

(The Extra fans them as they kiss.)

THE EXTRA. The camera loves them.

The camera doesn't see anyone else.

(Speaking of herself.)

So she is hired to play Anyone Else.

The Extra. Anyone Else is her specialty.

PENTHESILEA. Your lips are dry. Some grapes, my pet?

ACHILLES. Achilles belongs to no woman.

PENTHESILEA. Some grapes for my new lion!

(The Extra goes and returns instantly, her face obscured by a plate of grapes.)

THE EXTRA. An Extra has to be non-descript. An Extra has a whole arsenal of non-description at her disposal. Sometimes you'd catch her elbow in the corner of the frame, over the star's shoulder. She became a good listener.

THE FRAU. Cut! *(Breaking out of her Penthesilea character.)*

Who said you could talk to the camera?

THE EXTRA. I'm sorry.

THE FRAU. This is *my* story.

(She rips off her blonde wig and looks out toward the audience, where the cameras would be.)

I said CUT!

Scene 1

Off Camera.

(Lights out on all but the Extra.)

THE EXTRA. *(out)* It is my story too. Only she doesn't know it yet.

When the camera goes off, the star becomes smaller. Mortal. Everyone knows this. But few people know that when the Extra puts down her spear and steps off the sound stage and back into her life, she grows larger. She has a story too.

(Beat.)

The first person the Frau cast was herself.

(Light on the Frau.)

THE FRAU. Who else to play the Amazon queen?

THE EXTRA. Right away, a problem.

THE FRAU. Penthesilea was a blonde...

THE EXTRA. But the Frau was not.

THE FRAU. *(holding up the wig, eyeing it like an adversary)* It would be necessary to practice.

THE EXTRA. The next person she cast was Achilles.

But while he too was blonde...

(Light rises on the Man, in a dark coat now.)

THE MAN. She hired a dark-eyed man from the ghetto to play him.

THE EXTRA. ...So that no one on screen would be blonder than she.

THE MAN. And also because he came cheap. And because of his strong back. And because of the constellation of moles leading the eye down his strong back.

THE FRAU. *(salacious)* You are *very* talented.

THE MAN. That is what I am told.

THE FRAU. They say you have no formal training, but you have instincts.

THE MAN. *(taking a step back from her)* Everyone has instincts.

THE FRAU. You don't act like you want this job.

THE MAN. How do I act?

THE FRAU. Like I *owe* you the job.

THE MAN. What exactly is the job?

THE FRAU. The man who is my match.

Do you think you're up to it?

THE MAN. How will you pay me?

Everyone in the ghetto says: She has lost favor with the Minister of Propaganda. She is no longer playing with state money.

THE FRAU. I made the state's films with the state's money. Now I am making my own film. A love story inside a war story.

THE MAN. What will you pay me?

THE FRAU. I will pay you in fame.

(He scoffs.)

THE FRAU. I am offering you a steady job.

(Regarding the Star of David he wears:)

It may be good for you to keep busy.

(Light shifts. Everything accelerating now.)

THE EXTRA. Two months later, in the darkest age of the last century, she started filming her adaptation of *Penthesilea*.

(During the following, the Frau puts on the blonde wig.)

THE EXTRA. On a sound stage outside the great city, the Frau learned how to ride bareback, she learned to land a punch,

THE FRAU AS PENTHESILEA. She learned how to be blonde.

THE EXTRA. All for nothing. Of the 34 scenes in her screen-play, none were completed.

What you will see are mere scraps of image. Here. Watch. See what you can snatch from the cutting room floor.

THE FRAU. *(out)* Roll film!

Scene 2

On Camera.

THE GREEKS DECIDE TO OFFER THE AMAZONS AN ALLIANCE. PENTHESILEA REFUSES.

THE FRAU. The camera swoops over dunes and choked little rivers.

THE EXTRA. Settling on the Amazon army, a row of tiny specks in the desert.

THE FRAU. Tracking closer

THE EXTRA. And the armor

THE FRAU. Closer

THE EXTRA. The jewel on an elephant's brow

THE FRAU. Sound in

THE EXTRA. Tambourines!

THE FRAU. A feminine noise, strange to this war.
Close-up

THE MAN AS ACHILLES. Achilles turns his proud head toward the music.

THE FRAU. Closer-up

ACHILLES. Women of Amazonia! I offer you an alliance. Together we can defeat Troy!

THE FRAU. Cut to

THE EXTRA AS AMAZON #1. An Amazon takes aim with her slingshot – there will be no alliance!

THE FRAU. The camera, panning

AMAZON 1. The stone in flight

THE FRAU. Jump cut

ACHILLES. Achilles ducks

AMAZON 1. Too late!

ACHILLES. His helmet falls

THE FRAU, ACHILLES, AMAZON 1. Crash!

AMAZON 1. To the ground.

ACHILLES. His head suddenly naked

THE FRAU. Extreme close-up

ACHILLES. He

is

beautiful.

AMAZON 1. The Amazon queen makes her way through the crowd.

THE FRAU AS PENTHESILEA. *(breathless)* Who knew he'd be beautiful?

AMAZON 1. Her faithful army doesn't see the first symptoms of love on her face.

PENTHESILEA. Only the camera does.

ACHILLES. Achilles picks up his helmet, looking her in the eye the whole time.

PENTHESILEA. *(faux-innocent)* Did you drop something?

ACHILLES. He is proud

PENTHESILEA. Even in his humiliation

ACHILLES. He is *terribly* proud of himself.

THE FRAU. CUT!

(The Frau breaks character.)

Couldn't you make him a bit more beautiful? A bit more *proud*?

THE MAN. I'm trying.

THE FRAU. Like a lion, here, watch. *(She puffs out her chest.)* See my –

End of fragment.

Scene 3.

On Camera.

PENTHESILEA SPARES ACHILLES' LIFE IN BATTLE.

THE FRAU. Exterior. Day.

THE MAN AS ACHILLES. Achilles.

THE FRAU AS PENTHESILEA. And Penthesilea.

ACHILLES & PENTHESILEA. Spear to spear.

ACHILLES. You're new here.

PENTHESILEA. Here is new to me.

ACHILLES. You came to fight?

PENTHESILEA. I came to be queen of you.

We need to replenish our numbers.

Your manparts are useful to us.

THE EXTRA. Penthesilea appraises him like a piece of meat.

PENTHESILEA. In your country, are they all made like you?

THE EXTRA. The camera appraises him like a piece of statuary.

ACHILLES. Are they all made like *you*, in your country?

THE EXTRA. Something passes between them

ACHILLES & PENTHESILEA. In soft focus

THE EXTRA. But the Amazons only see their queen

PENTHESILEA. *(romantic)* Defenseless

ACHILLES. *(self-important)* With her mortal enemy.

(The Extra enters the scene as Amazon #2.)

THE EXTRA AS AMAZON 2. *(drawing her bow)* My queen, your mortal enemy!

PENTHESILEA. *(turning sharply to Amazon 2)* The Amazon who takes aim at Achilles is felled by an arrow.

AMAZON 2. *(hand flying to her throat)* Blood?

PENTHESILEA. Penthesilea rushes to comfort the dying woman.

AMAZON 2. From my own queen's quick quiver?

(*A bit of a pietà.*)

PENTHESILEA. *Shh,* my dear. My heroic dear. *Shh, shh.*
The pain won't last. The veins will spend their contents.
It's this hole in your throat that's the trouble.
How could you have known he was *my* prize.
You couldn't have known where your loyalties would get you.

(*Her focus shifts to the far horizon.*)

Your own blood is carrying you to the beds of all the empresses that ever lived. And your left breast is waiting for you there, marvelous, on a rose red cushion. The tip of my arrowhead has made you complete. *Shh, shh, shh.*

AMAZON 2. And the faithful Amazon dies in her arms...

(*wheezingly*) with a wheeze.

PENTHESILEA. (*dropping the Amazon's head*) Fetch me a shovel.

THE EXTRA. (*still on the ground, dead*) The soundtrack wells up, in place of tears in her eyes.

PENTHESILEA. Has anyone seen Achilles?

THE EXTRA. The camera dollies in close,
so close that we can see the perspiration on her brow.

PENTHESILEA. Has anyone seen Achilles?

THE EXTRA. ...As if we needed further evidence of her wicked little crush.

THE FRAU. And...Cut.

(*The Extra rubs her sore head. The Frau is pleased with herself.*)

Good.
Very good, everyone. *Very –*

End of fragment.

Scene 4

Off Camera.

THE EXTRA. Between takes, the Frau retreated to her office, where the journalists came to ask: Where had the film come from?

THE FRAU. *(poised, as if in an interview)* Penthesilea, the woman warrior. When I was at university, I looked for her everywhere in the ancient texts. In her first appearance, the epic *Aethiopis,* she is granted just two sentences:

THE EXTRA. 1. "The Amazon queen arrives to aid the Trojans in war."

2. "Achilles kills Penthesilea and the Trojans bury her."

THE FRAU. Her first appearance and already she is forgotten.

Then I discovered the play by Heinrich von Kleist, who revises both statements:

1. Penthesilea enters the war to aid no one but herself.

2. She kills Achilles and dirties her face with his blood.

Now here was a woman to be interested in.

Scene 5

On Camera.

ACHILLES' CHARIOT CRASHES.
THE AMAZONS BLOCK HIS WAY.

(Achilles holds the reins, taut, with nothing attached to them. Or perhaps they lead off into the wings? Stagey.)

THE MAN AS ACHILLES. Fly you my steady steeds, fly! I must escape her before I lose myself. I must escape myself.

THE FRAU. The camera lurching, hoof-high.

ACHILLES. She makes my heart stop. She makes my heart race. She has that effect. She has that affect.

THE FRAU. The camera, breakneck.

ACHILLES. She makes my tongue stop. She makes my tongue race, faster than my mind can think of words. But not faster than my chariot!

THE FRAU. At this speed, the camera can't tell the blue backdrop from the great desert sky.

ACHILLES. My men taken captive, yet I run! But wouldn't it be more cowardly to stay and kneel at her feet and call her Queen?

(The Extra, playing Amazon #3, steps forward and cuts his reins.)

THE EXTRA AS AMAZON 3. You're not going anywhere.

ACHILLES. And why not?

AMAZON 3. Because she has claimed you for her prize.

ACHILLES. I will fly on foot if I have to!

AMAZON 3. *(shouting after him, as he runs)* Your heart will not escape!

THE FRAU. Cut!

(Pause.)

Maybe if you were less corny?

THE EXTRA. I'm sorry.

THE FRAU. *(out)* Again.

ACHILLES' CHARIOT CRASHES.
THE AMAZONS BLOCK HIS WAY.

(Just as before:)

ACHILLES. My men taken captive, yet I run! But wouldn't it be more cowardly to stay and kneel at her feet and call her Queen?

THE EXTRA AS AMAZON 3. You're not going anywhere.

ACHILLES. And why not?

AMAZON 3. Because she has claimed you for her prize.

ACHILLES. I will fly on foot if I have to!

AMAZON 3. *(shouting after him)* Your heart will not esca – !

(Breaking character, as the Extra now.)

I'm sorry.

THE FRAU. Yes.

(Off Camera now:)

THE EXTRA. *(out, as if to the crew)* I'm sorry.

THE MAN. It's not her, it's the line.

THE FRAU. What?

THE EXTRA. He's sorry.

THE FRAU. WHAT?

THE EXTRA. *(cueing the Man)* He's *very* sorry.

THE MAN. I'm sorry.

(The Boy enters.)

THE BOY. Telegram, Ma'am?

(They all spin toward him. In plain clothes, he seems like a visitor from another planet.)

THE FRAU. Ten minutes, everyone.

THE BOY. It is from the Ministry of Culture.

THE FRAU. This should be sobering.

(As she opens the telegram, we see the **MINISTER OF PROPAGANDA** *in a pool of light. He speaks out.)*

THE MAN AS THE MINISTER OF PROPAGANDA. Dear Fraulein –

THE FRAU. The Minister was always a flatterer.

THE MINISTER OF PROPAGANDA. Some are saying: you'd do better to leave ancient history and portray our own country's great story, still being written. *Stop.*

THE FRAU. The Minister was always a Modernist.

THE MINISTER OF PROPAGANDA. Others are saying: you'd do better not to shelter Jews and homosexuals in the embrace of your fiction. *Stop.*

(This knocks the wind out of her. The Minister tips his hat.)

THE MINISTER OF PROPAGANDA. To your health, Fraulein.
(As his light winks out:)
Stop.

THE FRAU. Three sentences. The Minister was always cheap.

THE FRAU. Boy!

(The Boy takes out a pencil, paper.)

THE BOY. Ready ma'am.

THE FRAU. *(dictating; not heated, but quick and sharp)*
My dear sir *Stop*. There is no place for your war on my set *Stop*. My camera interested in a noble war *Stop*. My camera bored with your pomp and your circumstance *Stop*. My actors too busy to fill your work camps *Stop*. My actors too beautiful to fill your work camps *Stop*. No interest whatsoever in your grim telegrams *Stop*. I feed your telegrams to the horses for lunch *Stop*. I feed your telegrams to the ladies who lunch *Stop*. This wire already extravagant *Stop*. Stop sending *Stop*. Stop calling *Stop*. Stop *Stop*.

(To the Boy.)

That is all.

THE EXTRA. She knows the Ministry will not be pleased...

THE BOY. *(lingering)* Good evening then, ma'am.

THE EXTRA. ...But this is to be her masterpiece, and she won't have their fingerprints on it.

THE FRAU. What, you expect some kind of tip?

THE BOY. No ma'am.

THE FRAU. *(to the Extra)* Take him to the pantry. Give him a chocolate biscuit.

THE EXTRA. How old are you?

THE BOY. Twenty, ma'am.

THE FRAU. *(brightly)* No one is too old for a chocolate biscuit!

THE BOY. Good night, ma'am.

(He exits.)

THE EXTRA. He wanted *money*.

THE FRAU. There isn't any to spare.

THE EXTRA. *(under her breath)* Maybe if you wrote shorter telegrams...

THE FRAU. We are already over budget for the month.
Equipment Rental. Horses. *Actors.*
Tomorrow we shoot the first Patroclus scene and there is no Patroclus!

THE EXTRA. We could sell the crystal, if it comes to that.

THE FRAU. Do you think *you* could play a boy?

THE EXTRA. I played Hamlet in drama school.

THE FRAU. You do have a certain mannish way about you.

THE EXTRA. I played Don Juan, in trousers. The audience stood at the end!

THE FRAU. The stage is one thing, but the camera isn't nearly so forgiving.
Beautiful Patroclus, who Achilles loves like... a brother.

(The Frau looks at the Extra, scrutinizing. The Extra offers her face for observation – she blinks, prettily.)

We'll give it a try.

THE EXTRA. Thank you.

THE FRAU. *(cautionary)* This time, you'll have close-ups.

Scene 6

On Camera.

BACK AT THE CAMP, ACHILLES IS WELCOMED BY PATROCLUS.

THE FRAU. The camera circles the Greek campfire,
    shifting from light to desert dark.

THE MAN AS ACHILLES. Achilles cannot disguise the stars in
    his eyes

THE EXTRA AS PATROCLUS. His companion, Patroclus, wraps
    him in a blanket. Trying not to lose him to whatever
    force has possessed him.

THE FRAU. But the camera tells us he has already lost the
    battle:

PATROCLUS. Out of focus, he barely makes it into the frame.

THE FRAU. Instead, Achilles fills the screen:

ACHILLES. She is Aphrodite clad in Ares! She is a sheep in
    wolf's clothing!
    She is both sexes she is neithersex she is nethersex
    She is made of wolves and stars!

PATROCLUS. You want her.

ACHILLES. No.

PATROCLUS. You want to belong to her.

ACHILLES. No. She is a beast, she is a snake!

PATROCLUS. She makes you speak in metaphor.
    That can't be good.

ACHILLES. Only because she is less than human –
    The human words fall off her like arrows off well-made
    armor.

PATROCLUS. Then…we still belong to each other?

ACHILLES. Always.

PATROCLUS. But when he looks into Achilles' eyes,
    he sees *her* there

THE FRAU AS PENTHESILEA. Stretching like a tigress

ACHILLES. Deep in those two dark mirrors.

THE FRAU. (A very clever double exposure technique, which I invented.)

(Patroclus is stung.)

PATROCLUS. She's in you already.

ACHILLES. Patroclus, no.

PATROCLUS. She wants to blind you to anything else, to anyone else!

THE FRAU. Cut cut CUT!

(Off Camera now:)

THE MAN. *(to the Extra, under his breath)* She scares me.

THE FRAU. This isn't working.

THE EXTRA. *(under her breath)* Shhh. She can help you.

THE FRAU. You're not pretty enough.

We're going to need a real boy.

(The Frau stalks off.)

THE MAN. Why is she so terrible to you?

THE EXTRA. She's my sister.

(Pause)

THE MAN. The Frau is your *sister?*

THE EXTRA. I've been in twenty-seven of her films. I get to die in each one. Sometimes I die more than once in one film. It's my specialty.

THE MAN. Your specialty?

THE EXTRA. I've died by arrow, I've died by leprosy, gangrene, torn to pieces by angry mob, angry dogs, typhoon, starvation, walked the plank, thrown to sharks, mountain lion, mountain goat, mountain climbing accident. Guillotine. (I played a furious head without a body – did you know your head can live for thirty seconds without your body?) And the sword-and-sandal pictures: I died by locust swarm, asp to the breast, wrath of God. Cannonball, catapult, crucifixion.

I'll never have my name above the title but I'm the best there is at dying.

THE MAN. You have a talent for dying.

THE EXTRA. For dying *inconspicuously*, yes.

THE MAN. That isn't a talent I aspire to.

(Short pause)

THE EXTRA. She will keep you safe, I promise. She has already spoken to them on your behalf.

THE MAN. Them…

THE EXTRA. The men who make decisions. The men who have no trouble falling asleep at night.

THE MAN. What if you're wrong?

THE EXTRA. She is very useful to them. She makes their images. She can keep you safe.

THE MAN. Nowhere is safe.

THE EXTRA. Here, in her fantasy, it is safe. *(Beat.)* I know this all must seem…melodramatic at times. She is not a writer. She is not an acting teacher. But when you see it all up on the screen, you won't believe it. You won't *believe* it. It happens to me every time. Her genius is in what she keeps and what she throws to the cutting room floor. Nothing will end up in the frame that she doesn't want there. Not even Them.

But you must be useful to her, in turn.

THE MAN. And how can I be useful?

THE EXTRA. Be beautiful.

THE MAN. Is that all?

THE EXTRA. And act well. But more important, be beautiful.

Scene 7

Off Camera.

THE EXTRA. The Frau sinks into her favorite armchair, smoking one of her rare cigars.

THE FRAU. Thinking

and

thinking

and

thinking.

THE EXTRA. *(entering the scene)* The Extra swallows her pride.

THE FRAU. *(as if she's saying "nemesis")* Sister.

THE EXTRA. Sister, I have an idea.

THE FRAU. Speak.

THE EXTRA. What about the messenger boy?

The one who brings the telegrams?

THE FRAU. You mean

THE EXTRA. He might play your Patroclus.

He will be cheap. And he is not unattractive.

THE FRAU. Perhaps, if I hire him, the telegrams will stop coming?

THE EXTRA. Those big, dark eyes!

When he arrives on the set with your messages, the cameramen whisper:

(Like a secret password:) "Did you bring a little something for me?"

THE FRAU. How imprudent of them.

THE EXTRA. What do you mean?

THE FRAU. There are others, outside the arts, who are not as tolerant as you and me.

THE EXTRA. *(out)* She takes a big puff on her cigar, and those words seem to hang,

like the smoke,

in the air.

THE FRAU. Anything outside of God's design we can choose to abide or...not to abide.

THE EXTRA. What if God's design is not immediately apparent to us?

Is there anything in the world that isn't God's design?

THE FRAU. *("I seem to have touched a nerve")* You are very theological tonight.

THE EXTRA. Sometimes, I think you talk like them. I don't like it.

THE FRAU. You think I talk like –

THE EXTRA. Your former patrons.

THE FRAU. *Employers.*

THE EXTRA. I see you: Using the same camera angles you used to film the rallies. The special lens you built for seeing an entire army assembled. Only it is a different army this time.

THE FRAU. I invented those techniques. Why shouldn't I use them?

THE EXTRA. They are good for filming bodies, not people.

THE FRAU. What are you saying?

THE EXTRA. I am saying: I think you are making something that will please them.

(Pause.)

THE EXTRA. I am not trying to draw blood. I only want / you to –

THE FRAU. Why are you here, if you find my film so distasteful?

THE EXTRA. Because I think you are an artist, and some days even a great one. But –

THE FRAU. But –

THE EXTRA. With that, there comes a responsibility –

THE FRAU. "Responsibility!" Art is not responsible.

THE EXTRA. Why is that?

THE FRAU. Because, in art, beauty comes before justice.

THE EXTRA. I hear they are often the same thing, beauty and justice.

THE FRAU. In art?

    (She blows a ring of smoke.)

    I'm afraid they are almost never.

    (A knock from outside.)

THE FRAU. Enter.

    (The Boy comes in.)

THE BOY. Telegram, ma'am.

THE FRAU. *(looking to the Extra)* I see.

THE BOY. It is the Ministry.

    (Continuous into:)

Scene 8

Off Camera.

(As the Frau reads the telegram:)

THE EXTRA. She hadn't always dreaded the arrival of the Minister's telegrams.

But no one knew exactly what had passed between them. In interviews, she would say, simply

THE FRAU. Who can live in the past?

THE EXTRA. But if the journalists were patient, and they brought her a box of chocolate biscuits, they were sometimes rewarded.

THE FRAU. Years ago, when I was Fraulein not Frau,

I stood in the doorway of an important party.

The Minister of Propaganda was there.

(Light rises on the Minister of Propaganda, played by the Man. A German accent would be good.)

THE MAN AS THE MINISTER OF PROPAGANDA. ...In a smart tuxedo.

THE FRAU. This champagne is repellent, don't you think?

THE MINISTER OF PROPAGANDA. Do not pretend to be a sophisticate.

You are more alive than all these people.

I have seen your films.

THE FRAU. Ah, my little alpine adventures.

THE MINISTER OF PROPAGANDA. Every frame vibrates with energy.

You must direct a film of our upcoming rally.

THE FRAU. Your rallies are not for me.

I'm an actress at heart – I want nice parts to play.

THE MINISTER OF PROPAGANDA. What sort of parts interest you?

THE EXTRA. ...He says, ambiguously.

But she does not seem to notice:

THE FRAU. I have always wanted to play Penthesilea.
From Kleist's great drama.

THE MINISTER OF PROPAGANDA. Why Penthesilea?

THE FRAU. She is beautiful but fierce. She is headstrong.
She is a warrior but she puts love above everything
else.

(Short pause)

THE MINISTER OF PROPAGANDA. You have just described
yourself, Fraulein.

THE FRAU. *(visibly pleased, but trying to hide it)* Perhaps.

THE MINISTER OF PROPAGANDA. With one exception:
I would wager you never put love above anything.

THE FRAU. I do the work that must be done.
I can think of no other way to live my life.

THE MINISTER OF PROPAGANDA. Then we are the same, you
and me.

THE FRAU. We are *not* the same.

THE EXTRA. ...She says, tossing back the champagne.

THE FRAU. I am an artist.

THE MINISTER OF PROPAGANDA. Look how you pick a fight.

THE EXTRA. He says, sliding his hand down her back.

THE MINISTER OF PROPAGANDA. Look how you pick a fight.
You *are* an Amazon.

THE FRAU. *Sie sind nicht Achilles.*

THE EXTRA. ...She says. *(Translating)* "You are no Achilles."

(The Frau steps out of the scene.)

THE FRAU. *(poised again)* From then on, our relationship
was civil at best.

THE EXTRA. ...She would say in the interviews, many years
later.
After the war, it was necessary that they be adversaries.

THE FRAU. Often, it was much less than civil.

THE EXTRA. But the journalists sensed she was leaving some of the story on the cutting room floor:

(The Frau is pulled back into the scene.)

THE MINISTER OF PROPAGANDA. *(as before)* Then we are the same, you and me.

THE FRAU. *(as before)* We are *not* the same. I am an artist.

THE EXTRA. Perhaps she'd accepted his hand on her back.

THE MINISTER OF PROPAGANDA. Look how you pick a fight.

You *are* an Amazon.

THE FRAU. An Amazon with no army to command...

THE MINISTER OF PROPAGANDA. I will ask one more time, Fraulein.

Make a film of the upcoming rally:

You will have a queen's budget. You will have an army of underlings to command. When it is finished, you will have all the fame you need to make *Penthesilea.*

THE EXTRA. Perhaps she took another flute of champagne.

THE FRAU. The preparation, the editing: We are talking about years of my life.

THE MINISTER OF PROPAGANDA. Your Amazon queen will wait.

THE FRAU. You think?

I suspect she is impatient, like me.

THE EXTRA. Perhaps she took his arm and accepted his introductions to important people.

THE MINISTER OF PROPAGANDA. Actress, dancer, mountaineer – and now, the Ministry's chief directrix!

THE EXTRA. Perhaps she said her goodbyes and walked home,

the painful shoes dangling from her right hand.

Although it was late, she lay awake, thinking of the men she'd charmed and the new alliance she'd made.

Outside her window, the boots of soldiers went:

THE FRAU. Left-right, left-right

THE EXTRA. Over the stones of the Preiser Platz.

The Frau lay awake all night.

Haunted by the Minister saying...

THE MINISTER OF PROPAGANDA. "We are the same, you and me"

THE EXTRA. ...she started to dream up the film that would prove him wrong.

Scene 9

On Camera.

BACK AT THE CAMP, ACHILLES IS WELCOMED BY PATROCLUS.

(Repeated scene. With the Boy as Patroclus now. Much more chemistry with Achilles this time, and less camp.)

THE MAN AS ACHILLES. She is Aphrodite clad in Ares! She is a sheep in wolf's clothing!
She is both sexes she is neithersex she is nethersex
She is made of wolves and stars!

THE BOY AS PATROCLUS. *(simply, sadly)* You want her.

ACHILLES. No.

PATROCLUS. You want to belong to her.

ACHILLES. No. She is a beast, she is a snake!

PATROCLUS. She makes you speak in metaphor. That can't be good.

ACHILLES. Only because she is less than human –
The human words fall off her like arrows off well-made armor.

PATROCLUS. Then...we still belong to each other?

ACHILLES. Always.

THE FRAU. And again, the camera peers into Achilles' eyes

ACHILLES. But this time it sees only

THE BOY. Him, poised like a panther

THE MAN. Reflected in those two dark mirrors.

(The Frau is stung.)

THE FRAU. Cut Cut CUT! We have another problem.

THE MAN. What now.

THE FRAU. He's *too* beautiful.

THE BOY. I'm sorry.

THE FRAU. *(shouting off)* Make-up!

THE MAN. *(to the Boy)* Don't be sorry.

THE FRAU. *(shouting off)* Get him out of that eyeliner!
He's not the Queen of Sheba!

THE MAN. *(to the Boy)* You're doing very well.

THE FRAU. Give him a scar or something. Muddy his face.

THE BOY. *(to the Man)* Thank you.

THE FRAU. *(out)* I thought I said c –

End of fragment.

Scene 10

Off Camera.

THE EXTRA. The next day

THE MAN. *(to the Boy)* Hello

THE EXTRA. The Man eats his lunch at the edge of the grounds

THE MAN. I said Hello

THE EXTRA. And the Boy brings the telegrams

THE BOY. Hello

THE EXTRA. The messenger bag dusting his right thigh.

THE MAN. *(like a secret password)* Did you bring a little something for me?

THE BOY. Sorry.

THE MAN. You're asked that a lot.

THE BOY. Yes.

THE MAN. You are even darker than me. Are you Jewish?

THE BOY. My parents came from Romania.

THE MAN. Gypsies!

THE BOY. That is a word for us.

THE MAN. You don't wear an earring.

THE BOY. And I won't tell you the future.

THE MAN. But you know it?

THE BOY. Yes.

THE MAN. Do you read her messages?

(Pause)

THE BOY. Every day.

THE MAN. And they tell you about the future?

THE BOY. They tell me about the Frau.

THE MAN. And...

THE BOY. There is a place for her in the future, if she wants it.

THE MAN. Is there a place for us, in the future?

THE BOY. It doesn't take special powers to see what will happen to us.

THE MAN. We're safe here. As long as we're working.

THE BOY. You think so?

THE MAN. She told me.

THE BOY. You're trusting.

THE MAN. You're beautiful.

(The Man kisses him. Impulsively, but the kiss lasts.)

THE BOY. I don't do this.

THE MAN. Now you do.

THE BOY. Someone will see.

THE MAN. Then we'll tell them we're rehearsing.

(They kiss again.)

Scene 11

Off Camera.

THE EXTRA. Later that day

THE BOY. *(to the Frau)* Telegram, Ma'am.

THE EXTRA. In the Frau's chamber

THE FRAU. You are still delivering messages?

THE BOY. I need the money. You pay me with chocolate biscuits.

THE FRAU. You are late.

THE BOY. I'm sorry.

THE FRAU. The telegrams never come after noon.

THE BOY. I was held up. There are many messages today.

THE FRAU. Every day, the real world chatters on.

How am I supposed to imagine another world?

THE BOY. Why do you have to imagine another world?

THE FRAU. Where else will we go when this one ends?

(The Extra takes the telegram from the Boy.)

THE EXTRA. *(taking the telegram)* It's from Mummy.

THE FRAU. Mummy.

THE EXTRA. It's Mummy.

THE FRAU. *(shaken)* It's been so long.

THE EXTRA. *(out)* They have not spoken since Mummy bought her hot chocolate on the Strassengammer-platzenplatz

THE FRAU. And she told me Papa wouldn't stand for my playacting any longer

THE EXTRA. And she gave her a choice:

THE FRAU. To be with my family or become a star.

THE EXTRA. The rest is history.

(The Frau stares at the envelope.)

THE FRAU. I'm afraid.

THE EXTRA. Read it.

THE FRAU. What if Papa were sick, how could I continue my work?

THE EXTRA. Read it.

THE FRAU. And yet I must continue.

THE EXTRA. Read it!

THE FRAU. I think I will read it.

(We see **MUMMY** *in a pool of light as the Frau reads. She is played by the Man. [Nothing too broad please. Perhaps Mummy is a sort of late Jeanne Moreau type – husky voice, black lace veil.])*

THE MAN AS MUMMY. My little

my little

my little treasure *Stop.*

I know we haven't talked for thirteen years since I bought you hot chocolate on the Strassengammer-platzenplatz and you told me you would choose your playacting over your loving family but I hear from your sister that you're in the mountains in the great blue Tyrol and I thought you should come home because there is going to be a war here too there's no need to make one up! Your father is dying with a great big tumor in his knee and gallstones and kidney stones and all kinds of round strange stones inside him *Stop.* How did they get in there I wonder *Stop.* I know you will make the right choice this time *Stop.* You'd better *Stop.* Your loving mummy *Stop.*

(Pause)

THE FRAU. This is a very expensive telegram.

MUMMY. I sold my wedding ring to buy it. *(As her light winks out.)*

Stop.

(The Frau crumples the telegram in her fist.)

THE EXTRA. *(to the Boy)* I should want to tap out a reply.

THE BOY. Yes of course ma'am.

THE EXTRA. *(to the Frau)* Should I give them your regards?

THE FRAU. "The right choice this time."

She thinks I had a choice!

THE EXTRA. There is always a choice –

THE FRAU. Says the woman in charge of nothing and no one.

(Beat. Re: the telegram again.)

Rather unfair of her to bring up ancient history.

THE EXTRA. History is for bringing up.

THE FRAU. Must you always be an insurgent?

THE EXTRA. Must you always be a dictator?

BOTH. Yes.

(Pause)

THE EXTRA. *(tenderly, taking a different tack)* You were his favorite.

You would give up the chance to see him again?

THE FRAU. I can see him in my memory, clear as a newsreel. I would prefer the memory to...maudlin fumblings.

THE EXTRA. Yes, it won't be edited to perfection. Yes, there will be wasted words. Bad takes. We will hold Papa's hand and watch the light leave his eyes.

THE FRAU. We will not.

(Short pause)

THE EXTRA. What should I tell them?

THE FRAU. Tell them my work is all-consuming.

Tell them I am unable to leave the set.

THE EXTRA. Then I'll tell them the truth.

Scene 12

On Camera.

ACHILLES GOES TO THE AMAZON CAMP IN PURSUIT OF PENTHESILEA.

THE EXTRA. The German mountains do their best to impersonate the Trojan desert:

THE MAN AS ACHILLES. Achilles travels on foot, under the night sky.

THE FRAU. (My blue-velvet opera cape, stretched wide.)

ACHILLES. The sand still burning from the heat of the day. At the mouth of a great cave...

THE FRAU. (Aluminum foil over chicken wire.)

ACHILLES. Achilles spots a raging campfire.

THE FRAU. (Shreds of yellow silk blown by a fan.)

ACHILLES. While the Amazons sleep, a lone figure leans over the fire, as if deciphering the next day's battle plans in the jumping flame.

PENTHESILEA. *(spinning around)* Who goes there?

ACHILLES. The son of a goddess.

The servant of your beauty.

PENTHESILEA. Why have you come?

THE EXTRA. *(as she plays one of the sleeping Amazons)*

(But something isn't quite right.)

ACHILLES. Why does a man visit a woman alone?

PENTHESILEA. To challenge her to a duel?

THE EXTRA. (The shadow cast by the "fire" is too steady.)

ACHILLES. Do you value yourself so little?

PENTHESILEA. On the contrary:

When men are taken with me, they are often struck speechless.

The very agility of your tongue betrays a campaign of flattery.

THE EXTRA. (The rocks of the "cave" too shiny.)

PENTHESILEA. I challenge you to a contest of spears!

ACHILLES. I would not want to tear that beautiful breast.

THE EXTRA. (The "moon" proclaims itself too loudly.)

THE FRAU. Cut!

THE MAN. What

(Off Camera now:)

THE FRAU. Ten minutes.

(The Man leaves, shaking his head.)

THE FRAU. I must have been mad. We need location shots! We need Africa! We need sand and rock and fire! I've been making an airless thing, a dead thing.

THE EXTRA. There are nine cameramen. There are a hundred blonde horsewomen.

How do you propose we get to Africa?

THE FRAU. *(small, almost bashful)* Planes?

THE EXTRA. Will you ask the Ministry for planes? When we are at the brink of war?

THE FRAU. If we use the Ministry's planes, it will be a Ministry film.

THE EXTRA. What will that mean?

THE FRAU. They will place their symbol on the Greek helmets.

They will want marches for the soundtrack.

They will try to make it a film about war, not a film about love.

(Short pause)

THE EXTRA. You are making a film about love?

Scene 13

On Camera.

COMBAT SCENES BETWEEN
THE THREE ARMIES.

THE EXTRA. The next day,
she shoots everything in close-up:

THE FRAU. Closer.
. I can still see our weak Northern sun.
Closer!

THE MAN AS ACHILLES. The sweat on their backs!

THE FRAU. Tighter

THE EXTRA AS AMAZON #4. The bright sand, like jewels, in
their hair!

THE FRAU. Jump cut

ACHILLES. The whip at the horse's –

THE FRAU. Jump cut

ACHILLES. The wheels of his –

THE FRAU. Jump cut

AMAZON 4. *(wielding a spear)* An Amazon spear between the
spokes!

THE FRAU.	**ACHILLES.**
And the camera crashes toward the ground!	And the chariot crashes toward the ground!

AMAZON 4. Earth / under

ACHILLES. Under wheel / over

AMAZON 4. Over foot / under

ACHILLES. Under hoof.

THE FRAU. Crushed under the horse, a nameless Amazon
hisses:

AMAZON 4. Have you forgotten the Queen's challenge?
Would the world's greatest hero run from the contest

of spears?

THE FRAU. Instead of her face, the camera focuses on the cracked earth behind her.

THE EXTRA. Suddenly, a cameraman's foot dirties the edge of the frame.

THE FRAU. Cut!

End of fragment.

Scene 14

Off Camera.

(The Man with the Boy, who has a telegram.)

THE BOY. Do we dare?

THE MAN. I've always wanted to see you tell the future.

(The Boy opens it. The Man looks over his shoulder.)

THE BOY. *(reading the telegram with much pomp)* "My Esteemed Friend,"

THE MAN. Ooh, "Friend?"

THE BOY. *(faux formality)* May I continue?

THE MAN. Please.

THE BOY. "My Esteemed Friend,
I will submit your request to the Minister of Defense *Stop.* Two planes to fly six actors and a skeleton crew of four to Cairo *Stop.* You would retain control, as requested, but I will approve final cut personally *Stop.* Confident your always-fine work will meet our standards *Stop.* To your health, Fraulein. *Stop.*"

(Pause.

The Boy looks up from the telegram.)

THE BOY. Do you think they're fucking?

THE MAN. Don't be disgusting.

THE BOY. "My Esteemed Friend..."

THE MAN. My Friend means fucking.
Esteemed Friend means "I *hope* we'll fuck."

THE BOY. Well, My Friend...

(The Man grins. Quick kiss.)

It looks like you're going to Africa.

THE MAN. You mean *we're* going to Africa.

THE BOY. She won't take me.

THE MAN. She knows there wouldn't be a film without you.

THE BOY. I hope you're right.

THE MAN. Cairo, just think! We can sit in the sun. We can smoke hashish. When the film is done, we'll go off to the desert...find some well-appointed cave and wait for the planes to leave. We don't ever have to come back to this country and its future.

(They kiss.)

(During the following, from another part of the stage, the Frau slowly turns her head to see them.)

THE EXTRA. Three stories up, through the leaves of the elm tree,

Behind the closed blinds of her apartment,

The Frau watches them.

Scene 15

On Camera.

ACHILLES TELLS PATROCLUS THAT HE WILL DUEL WITH THE AMAZON QUEEN.

THE FRAU. *Wide* lens, to amplify the distance between them.

THE BOY AS PATROCLUS. What if you fall to her spear?

THE MAN AS ACHILLES. I am more than a match for her.

PATROCLUS. That is not what I fear –

THE FRAU. The camera circling Achilles.

PATROCLUS. I'm afraid you will allow her to win.

ACHILLES. She is my destiny.

THE FRAU. Circling his heroic torso, 'til it finds the face of Patroclus:

PATROCLUS. Spangled with tears.

ACHILLES. Dry your eyes, boy.

Everything on this black earth must come to an end.

PATROCLUS. Not this. We are meant to be constellations!

We are meant to hang together in the sky!

THE FRAU. The camera comes to rest on both men.

(The following at a low whisper, out of character, while they continue to hold heroic poses. The Frau doesn't notice and continues filming.)

THE BOY. *(whisper)* Soon we will do this for real.

THE MAN. *(whisper)* What do you mean?

THE FRAU. The image sharpens

The focus deepens

The composition settles.

THE BOY. *(whisper)* You know what I mean.

THE MAN. *(whisper)* I will talk to her.

THE FRAU. The two men stand at either edge of the frame, like the fine white columns of the Acropolis.

THE MAN. *(whisper)* I will persuade her.

THE FRAU. Most cunningly,
   focus shifts from their bodies to the desert beyond

THE BOY. *(whisper)* How will you persuade her?

THE FRAU. And the open desert becomes the uncrossable
   distance between two souls.

THE MAN. *(whisper)* Don't be stupid.

THE BOY. *(whisper)* Don't be a whore.

THE FRAU. CUT!
   You are, what, chatting?

THE MAN. No.

THE FRAU. Your lips were moving.

THE BOY. I'm sorry.

THE FRAU. There are no lines!

THE MAN. We were improvising.

THE FRAU. All I need in this scene is your bodies.
   Your bodies will tell the story.
   Your bodies and the camera.

Scene 16

On Camera.

PENTHESILEA FALLS TO ACHILLES IN BATTLE. SHE IS UNAWARE OF WHAT IS HAPPENING AROUND HER.

THE FRAU. P.O.V. shot, ground level.

THE MAN AS ACHILLES. The boots of the advancing Greeks are upon her.

THE FRAU. Although she is unconscious, the camera still sees with her eyes:

A thousand men against the desert sky.

THE EXTRA. (The same wide lens that filmed the armies at the rally.)

THE FRAU. Just when her fate seems certain, the hero speaks:

ACHILLES. He leaves this place a shadow, whoever lays a hand upon my queen!

THE FRAU. Cut to an Amazon in the front lines, whispering:

THE EXTRA AS AMAZON #5. Can it be, love hast turned him against his own people?

ACHILLES. I will take this splendid woman back to Athens with me.

The rest of you may stay and fight for Helen, who pales in comparison.

THE FRAU. The camera swoops up to him: He seems so tall!

THE EXTRA. (The same angle that captured the Führer at his podium.)

ACHILLES. He leaves this place a shadow, whoever tries to stop me!

THE FRAU AS PENTHESILEA. Finally, the queen stirs.

ACHILLES. Rise, lady.

PENTHESILEA. I live…

But why?

ACHILLES. So that you can be my queen,

If you will have me as your king.

PENTHESILEA. My enemy, also my king?

ACHILLES. Excellent woman, I will live out my life in the fetters of your beauty.

But first, tell me your name.

PENTHESILEA. Names can be forgotten.

If you forgot my name, could you still find my image in yourself?

Can you still see me when you shut your eyes?

(He shuts his eyes.)

ACHILLES. You are so beautiful.

PENTHESILEA. Then my name is Penthesilea.

ACHILLES. You are so beautiful, Penthesilea.

(His eyes still shut. She begins to touch him on the face, the lips.)

PENTHESILEA. She doesn't need to ask his name.

ACHILLES. It is known in every country with a language.

THE FRAU. Cut.

Yes. Print it! Print –

End of fragment.

Scene 17

Off Camera.

(The Frau in her armchair, smoking a cigar.)

THE EXTRA. For the first time, the Man visits the Frau in her quarters.

THE FRAU. Speak.

THE MAN. It's Stefan.

THE FRAU. *(pretending not to know)* Stefan…

THE MAN. The boy who brings your telegrams.

The boy with five scenes in your magnum opus.

THE FRAU. Oh yes, the pretty pretty boy.

THE MAN. What if he were to come with us?

THE FRAU. To Africa.

THE MAN. You see everything that's happening. You know what he is. Let him come with us.

THE FRAU. You are the leading man.

Why should you intervene on behalf of a super-numerary?

THE MAN. Because he acts well.

THE FRAU. You lie very badly for an actor.

I ask you again: Why should you intervene on his behalf?

THE MAN. Because we.

Because he and I –

THE FRAU. And you're asking me to reward an abomination?

THE MAN. I'm asking you to take him with us. I am asking you to save him.

THE FRAU. And I am telling you I can't.

THE MAN. You don't really believe it's an abomination.

You put it in your adaptation – Patroclus isn't even *in* the Kleist play.

THE FRAU. I added him to deepen the emotional journey.

THE MAN. *(bitterly)* It has *worked*.

THE FRAU. You shouldn't have these distractions.
Perhaps that's why your performance has been so dissipated.

THE MAN. I will do better.

THE FRAU. You had such potential when I found you.
Now, the love scenes, there is barely a flicker behind your eyes.

THE MAN. What If I were to...find that flicker?

(He moves in to kiss her, but the Frau turns her cheek to him.)

THE FRAU. I don't believe you.

THE MAN. I'm acting as hard as I can.

THE FRAU. You're not behaving like a man who wants something from me.

THE MAN. How does such a man behave?

(The Frau pushes him slowly to his knees.)

THE FRAU. Ask me again.

THE MAN. How does such a man behave?

(The Frau pushes him onto his stomach.)

THE FRAU. Ask me again.

(Blackout.)

Roll film!

Scene 18

On Camera.

THE GREAT LOVE SCENE BETWEEN PENTHESILEA AND ACHILLES.

THE FRAU. Interior. Night.

(The following as a kind of foreplay:)

ACHILLES. Mosquitoes buzzing, wolves howling

PENTHESILEA. Incense censing

ACHILLES. Vaseline on the lens.

THE FRAU. *(shouting off)* More Vaseline on the lens!

ACHILLES. Candles craven in the desert wind.

(As we saw before in the Prologue:)

PENTHESILEA. *(smoldering)* Let me be food for your ravenous dogs.

Let me be breakfast.

Let me be dust.

ACHILLES. *(smoldering)* Let me trail like a corpse behind your flashing-hooved horses.

Let me be baggage.

Let me be ballast.

PENTHESILEA. Let me be cinders.

ACHILLES. Let me be ash.

Let me be nothing.

PENTHESILEA. Let *me* be nothing.

ACHILLES. No, me!

(They kiss.)

PENTHESILEA. Some grapes, my pet?

ACHILLES. Achilles belongs to no woman.

PENTHESILEA. *(shouting off)* Some grapes for my new lion!

(The Extra enters the scene as Amazon #6, her face

obscured by a plate of grapes. Achilles takes one of the grapes and poises it over his mouth.)

PENTHESILEA. Wait, my love – caution.

(She snaps her fingers and Amazon 6 tastes a grape. She is immediately stricken, doubled over.)

AMAZON 6. Poison?

ACHILLES. *(to Penthesilea, paying the Extra no mind)* Who would do such a thing?

PENTHESILEA. *(paying her no mind)* They know you're here with me – it can only be them.

ACHILLES. Who?

PENTHESILEA. The High Priestesses.

Powerful Amazons who would challenge this... attachment.

(Amazon 6 finally dies in agony, the grapes spilling onto the floor.)

ACHILLES. I fear no one in this world but you.

You, who hold my heart between your teeth.

PENTHESILEA. This is no time for metaphor. You aren't safe here. Go back to your Greeks. Go back to your Boy. Go back before something terrible –

End of fragment.

Scene 19

Off Camera.

(In a quiet corner of the set, the Boy approaches the Man.)

THE MAN. I talked to her.

THE BOY. I'm scared to ask.

(The Man looks impassive for a second, then smiles.)

THE BOY. Yes?

THE MAN. Yes.

(They embrace.)

THE BOY. What did you say to her?

THE MAN. Never mind that.

THE BOY. *(playful, jostling him)* What did you say!

THE MAN. It was a…masterpiece of flattery.

THE BOY. You are always the seducer.

(They are about to kiss. Suddenly the Extra is there.)

THE EXTRA. She's asking for you.

THE BOY. Me?

THE EXTRA. She needs you in costume for the Rose Festival.

THE BOY. *(to the Man)* My big scene.

THE MAN. *(squeezing his hand)* You'll be fine.

(The Boy exits. Short pause.)

THE MAN. Why do you look at me like that?

THE EXTRA. Be careful.

THE MAN. She already knows.

THE EXTRA. Yes.

But it will be better if you are discreet.

(The Extra starts to exit…)

THE MAN. You would say that.

(…but this stops her.)

THE EXTRA. What does that mean?

THE MAN. Why do you always go back to your room?

THE EXTRA. Why do I –

THE MAN. I see the light on in your room, late. Why don't you ever go out dancing with the rest of them? Why don't you go out looking for men, like the other Amazons? Do you have...someone?

(*Pause.*)

THE EXTRA. Once, I did.

THE MAN. What happened to her?

(*Pause.*)

THE EXTRA. Times are not the same anymore.

THE FRAU. (*from off*) Sister!

THE MAN. Does she know?

THE EXTRA. I have to go.

Scene 20

On Camera.

THE ROSE FESTIVAL:
THE AMAZON PRIESTESSES, ROSE MAIDENS, AND CAPTURED GREEKS.

THE FRAU. Rose petals fill the air. Rose petals blind the camera.

THE EXTRA AS AMAZON # 7. The Amazons dance a feverish victory dance!

THE FRAU AS PENTHESILEA. But a lone figure remains still, in the center of the frame.

AMAZON 7. *(still dancing)* My queen, do you not enjoy the festivities?

PENTHESILEA. It is foolish to celebrate when Achilles rides free!

THE EXTRA. she says, while a voiceover tells the truth:

PENTHESILEA. *(recorded voiceover, her lips not moving – during this, the Amazon dances in slow motion)*
How can I fight the very man who holds my heart captive?

THE EXTRA AS AMAZON 7. Forgive me, my lady, but can even you find the immortal's one weakness?

PENTHESILEA. Get out of my sight!

(The Extra exits, head hanging.)

PENTHESILEA. *(aloud now)* How can I fight the very man who holds my heart captive?

(The Extra re-enters as Amazon #8, with Patroclus in chains.)

AMAZON 8. My queen. This prisoner knows Achilles!

(She throws Patroclus at the foot of the queen.)

He stays with the great man in his tent.

PENTHESILEA. Speak, boy!

THE BOY AS PATROCLUS. I know Achilles' weakness, yes. But it is my honor to keep it secret from those who would do him harm.

AMAZON 8. Tear the secret out of him!

(We hear the canned cries of other Amazons: "Destroy him! Bleed him! Cut off his arms! See if love will save him then!" Penthesilea raises her hand to silence them, looking out.)

PATROCLUS. Do as you like. I will not speak.

PENTHESILEA. Why do you martyr yourself?

PATROCLUS. Because I love him.

THE EXTRA. And Penthesilea rises from her throne, Like a great bird stirred from sleep:

PENTHESILEA. "Love."

THE EXTRA. Close-up on her mouth, pronouncing the strange new word.

PENTHESILEA. *(almost inaudible)* "Love?"

PATROCLUS. Yes, love can make the greatest suffering light as air.

THE EXTRA. She tries to hide him in the background, in soft focus...

PATROCLUS. You can end my life, but I am still closer to him than you will ever be.

THE EXTRA. ...But even with his face dirtied, all the beauty on screen belongs to him.

PATROCLUS. Forgive me, queen. I will tell you nothing.

PENTHESILEA. Then you are no longer useful to us.
Kill him.

AMAZON 8. Of course, my queen.

(Penthesilea turns out for a close-up.)

PENTHESILEA. *(recorded voiceover)* But, can even death kill such a love as this?

THE FRAU. Cross fade from her face, pensive

THE MAN AS ACHILLES. To Achilles, riding full force toward his destiny.

THE FRAU. And…Cut. (***Off Camera now:***)

I think that is all for today.

(Everyone starts to leave.)

THE FRAU. Sister.

THE EXTRA. Yes?

THE MAN. *(to the Boy)* What does she have you wearing?

THE BOY. "Fetters."

THE FRAU. *(to the Extra)* Get us a table at the inn.

THE BOY. *(to the Man)* You like?

THE MAN. I like.

THE EXTRA. *(to the Frau)* Steak and potatoes?

THE FRAU. Very rare.

THE MAN. *(whispering to the Extra)* I think she forgot "please."

THE FRAU. *(to the Boy)* You, stay!

THE BOY. Stay?

(The Man winks at him. Then the Frau and the Boy are alone.)

THE BOY. Ma'am?

THE FRAU. You are good. You are not an actor – but, you are a very easy person to watch. I have been watching you.

THE BOY. *(unsure if this is a complement)* Thank you.

THE FRAU. *("no, it is not a complement")* I have been watching you.

(Pause.)

THE BOY. What do you see?

THE FRAU. From my window in the inn I see the sun come over the mountains.

I see the geese gather by the lake and

I see the private little movie you are making together.

(Pause.)

THE BOY. It is there, in your film, what we are doing.

It is in your own film.

THE FRAU. Achilles and Patroclus are old *companions*.

THE BOY. It is between the lines.

It is in the close-ups, not the words.

And close-ups are what you do best.

THE FRAU. What are you saying?

THE BOY. I am saying: this is the story you are telling.

I hope your Esteemed Friend will approve.

(Pause)

THE FRAU. If you leave at once – If you leave the set at once, you can walk back to Bucharest without a triangle to wear.

THE BOY. But I thought –

THE FRAU. If you leave tonight, while he sleeps, he can continue to work for me. That is my gift to you.

THE BOY. And if I don't leave?

THE FRAU. If you leave tonight, while he sleeps, I will give you a hundred marks for your work and you can buy all the chocolate biscuits in creation.

THE BOY. Why do you hate me?

THE FRAU. Because you have stolen my film.

Scene 21

Off Camera.

THE EXTRA. The next day, a boy with blonde hair delivers her telegrams.

THE FRAU. *(looking at the envelope)* News of Africa, I hope!

THE EXTRA. She gives him ten pfennigs, instead of chocolate.

(The Frau reads. Light up on the Minister of Propaganda.)

THE MINISTER OF PROPAGANDA. Esteemed Friend,
Share this with no one *Stop*. We cannot authorize travel to Africa due to imminent conflict *Stop*. I urge you to stay in the country until otherwise informed *Stop*. There are greater things afoot than even your camera can envision *Stop*.

THE EXTRA. What is it?

THE FRAU. It's nothing. An invitation to a banquet.
They want to give me an award.

THE EXTRA. Any news about the planes?

THE FRAU. Soon, he says. *(She realizes this isn't enough.)*
Really, how long do they expect me to shoot close-ups?

THE EXTRA. What will you do about Patroclus?

THE FRAU. He only had one more scene to film. *(With ceremony:)*
I was hoping that *you* might be up to the challenge.

THE EXTRA. Don't you think people will notice the difference?

THE FRAU. The lighting, the camera angles – I still have a few tricks up my sleeve!

THE EXTRA. But, when he sees me dressed in Stefan's costume –

THE FRAU. *(a sudden realization)* It will be beautiful.

THE EXTRA. I couldn't do that to him.

THE FRAU. Of course you can. This, sister, is what we call a break.

The big death scene: Finally, a challenge worthy of your talent.

Scene 22

On Camera.

ACHILLES FINDS PATROCLUS, MORTALLY WOUNDED.

THE FRAU. P.O.V. shot, looking into the sky. The vultures circling, hungry.
Sound in:

THE MAN AS ACHILLES. The hooves of his fastest steed, galloping to the rescue.

THE FRAU. Close-up

ACHILLES. Begone, princes of filth! You'll not feast today.

(The Extra turns over, revealing her face. For the first time, the Man sees that it isn't the Boy. He struggles to stay in character.)

THE EXTRA. The vultures scatter,
revealing the Extra in Patroclus's costume.

(Pause.)

ACHILLES. My boy, who has done this to you?

THE EXTRA AS PATROCLUS. *(barely able to speak)* Achilles?

ACHILLES. Don't try to speak. I'm here now.

(Achilles cradles Patroclus.)

THE EXTRA. She tries her best to hide her face.

THE FRAU. The entire scene filmed over her shoulder.

ACHILLES. This wound. It is the work of an Amazon blade.

PATROCLUS. *(speaking with great effort)* Old friend…

ACHILLES. Rest, my boy.

PATROCLUS. Old friend, heed this warning.

THE FRAU. Cut to

PATROCLUS. His fist opens, slowly

THE FRAU. The camera peers into his hand. Extreme

·   close-up on

PATROCLUS. A wild rose

 Crushed

 Like a bloodclot.

THE FRAU. And the noble boy dies in his arms.

ACHILLES. Patroclus.

 Old companion.

THE EXTRA. And though he looks down at me,

 that boy is still reflected in his eyes.

ACHILLES. I understand this warning.

 But even your death cannot free me from her.

 I must away to her. For there is no other place for

 me –

 (Pause. As the Man now:)

 I can't.

THE FRAU. Cut.

THE MAN. *(to the Frau)* Where is he.

THE FRAU. *(out)* CUT!

 (Off camera now. Rapidly:)

THE MAN. What have you done.

THE FRAU. What do you mean what have / I –

THE MAN. *(overlapping)*

What have you done with him.

THE FRAU. It seems he left during the night. No one saw
 him. *(Looking at the Extra)* What could we do but recast
 the part?

THE MAN. We had an agreement.

THE FRAU. I told you. I don't know where / he –

THE MAN. I DON'T BELIEVE YOU.

 (Pause.

 Then the following, rapidly:)

THE MAN. I will go back.

THE EXTRA. No.

THE MAN. I will find him.

THE FRAU. Ah, the rigors of love.

THE MAN. WHAT DO YOU KNOW ABOUT LOVE.

THE EXTRA. Gentle.

THE MAN. Someone who tells a love story by drawing blood.

THE FRAU. You are endangering yourself.

THE MAN. You're so good at filming me like a statue.
Make your film with statues.

THE FRAU. Go then. Go!
If you're fast you can snatch some of the film,
before they sweep him off the cutting-room floor.

(Pause.)

(The Man spits at her feet as he leaves.)

Scene 23

On Camera.

PENTHESILEA RETURNS TO REALITY, AFTER KILLING ACHILLES IN A FIT OF MADNESS.

(The Frau describes the camera's movements around her face – She is in the scene at the same time. Barely moving, offering her face for a beautiful close-up...)

THE FRAU. The camera first observes her through the parting dust.

Something is wrong. She is too still.

The woman who lives her life drawn like a bow,

suddenly still as a knife in the dirt.

Although her face is without expression, the camera's attention seems to change it: Cut from her face to the blood on her hands. Cut back, and the blank face seems to reveal something new underneath. We seem to see the moment when again she is more woman than beast. When she realizes what she's done.

The blood on her hands runs black and white.

The blood at her mouth.

Not

Her

Blood

Whose

Blood.

The camera, still now. As still as she.

Nothing moves, except something behind her eyes.

The delusions hemorrhaging from her head.

(The Extra enters quickly with a newspaper.)

THE EXTRA. Sister, read.

THE FRAU. We are filming.

THE EXTRA. *(out)* Cut!

THE FRAU. *I* say cut.

Cut!

Off camera now:

THE EXTRA. Read.

(As the Frau reads the newspaper, a projection comes up, in the manner of the scene headings:)

GERMANY INVADES POLAND

THE EXTRA. Now you understand?

THE FRAU. Yes.

THE EXTRA. Given the circumstances –

THE FRAU. Yes, the film –

THE EXTRA. No, not / the film –

THE FRAU. The film is more necessary than ever.

THE EXTRA. We are at *war* –

THE FRAU. The world needs art, especially in wartime. When art fails to make beauty, to help us understand the world –

THE EXTRA. Is that what you do? Help us understand the world?

THE FRAU. I locate perfection and I put it in the center, and anything less stays at the edge of the frame! It's my job!

THE EXTRA. It *was* your / job.

THE FRAU. Others, they make it their job to locate imperfection and snuff it. But I prefer to say "This is beautiful" or I say / "This is not so beautiful."

THE EXTRA. You sound like them! –

THE FRAU. I say "This is ideal" or I say "This is not / ideal"

THE EXTRA. You sound like them! –

THE FRAU. I am telling another story!

An ancient story. Heroes. Beauty. Love.

Are these things useful to them?

THE EXTRA. – .

THE FRAU. How can I not be useful to them!

(Accelerating now:)

THE EXTRA. Put down your camera.

THE FRAU. I can't do that.

THE EXTRA. Then you are an accomplice.

THE FRAU. No.

THE EXTRA. You held that boy's life in your arms and you dropped him.

You are no better than them.

THE FRAU. "Accomplice." You are the *ultimate* accomplice. Always *observing*. Ordering my steak. Hiding in my shadow, as the rest of your kind are identified.

(Pause)

THE EXTRA. What does that mean, my kind?

THE FRAU. Those outside of God's design.

(Pause)

Yes. It is written on your face. You aberration. You *sister*. It is written in all of your performances. You amateur.

(The Extra winces, her hand touching her brow.)

THE EXTRA. Oh –

THE FRAU. What

THE EXTRA. My –

My –

THE FRAU. Your what

(The Extra has dropped to her knees.)

THE EXTRA. I think it's my

THE FRAU. What!

THE EXTRA. My head it's my

THE FRAU. What do you mean your

THE EXTRA. I don't… know or I'd

THE FRAU. What's wrong with your head

THE EXTRA. Behind my eyes –

THE FRAU. I don't know what to do –

THE EXTRA. Like a,

like a –

THE FRAU. What should I –

THE EXTRA. Pain

THE FRAU. Marta?

> (*The Extra convulses. Unlike her on-camera death scenes, it is awkward, unbeautiful, scary.*)

THE FRAU. Marta! God!

Someone! Help!

> (*The Extra lies very still.*)

Marta?

> (*Pause.*
>
> *Then, suddenly:*)

THE EXTRA. You believed me.

THE FRAU. *What?*

> (*The Extra stands up, brushes herself off.*)

THE EXTRA. You *believed* me. You said my name!

THE FRAU. Are you mad?

THE EXTRA. *(wild, invigorated)* You never say my name, and now you use it like a magic word!

"Marta." You see? Every one of us has a name.

THE FRAU. What are you talking about.

THE EXTRA. Every one of us who takes an arrow through the throat. Every one of them who disappears during the night, all of the Extras. Why don't you point your camera at them?

> (*Short pause*)

SPEAK.

THE FRAU. *(still rattled)* That was very...realistic.

THE EXTRA. You've taught me one thing: how to die.

THE FRAU. And yet you're still here.

THE EXTRA. What do you mean?

THE FRAU. *(grave)* The others, they died better.

Scene 24

On Camera.

PENTHESILEA'S GREAT SCENE OF DESPAIR. SHE IS VISITED BY THE GODDESS OF LOVE.

THE FRAU. Deserted by the crew, her camera sits alone on a tripod.

Her camera, once agile, is rooted stupidly to the ground.

But it still sees

(As Penthesilea now:)

The pain.

Ares, God of War, split me in two with one of your thunderbolts.

End the pain.

THE BOY AS THE GODDESS OF LOVE. But it is not Ares who answers her prayers.

It is the Goddess of Love.

THE FRAU AS PENTHESILEA. Go away.

THE GODDESS OF LOVE. Child. You summoned me and now I've come.

PENTHESILEA. I didn't ask for you, I asked for my father, the god of war.

THE GODDESS OF LOVE. For one such as you, Love and War are forever entwined.

PENTHESILEA. Poetry can't help me any more.

THE GODDESS OF LOVE. Poetry can always help.

Where does it hurt.

PENTHESILEA. Go away.

THE GODDESS OF LOVE. I can't hear you.

PENTHESILEA. YOU'RE THE ONE WHO GOT ME INTO THIS MESS AND NOW I WILL THROW MYSELF INTO THE RIVER SCAMANDER.

YOU'RE THE CAUSE. YOU'RE THE –

(The Goddess of Love holds up her hand, gently, and Penthesilea is calmed as if by magic.)

THE GODDESS OF LOVE. Tell me, child. Where does it hurt?

(Without moving anything but her arm, Penthesilea indicates her head, her missing left breast, her groin.)

PENTHESILEA. Pain.

THE GODDESS OF LOVE. What can I do?

PENTHESILEA. Nothing.

THE GODDESS OF LOVE. But Aphrodite sings a wicked little lullaby

PENTHESILEA. And the soft notes fall on her like snowflakes:

THE GODDESS OF LOVE. *(singing)*

Lay your pretty head in the dust

And when you wake, you'll have an oceanfull of peacocks.

Take another drink of dust

And when you wake, you'll have a desertfull of trout.

Lay your pretty head in the dust

And dream of red revenge and bloodknots

And tribal beats and love-me-nots.

THE FRAU. And…cut.

THE GODDESS OF LOVE. Why do you always shout "Cut," just when the scene is getting interesting?

THE FRAU. I said Cut!

THE GODDESS OF LOVE. Don't you wonder what would happen if the camera kept running?

THE FRAU. Who are you.

THE BOY. *(breaking character)* Are you afraid it might find something real?

THE FRAU. This isn't in the script. None of this is in the script.

THE BOY. There isn't a script any more.

THE FRAU. Cut.

THE BOY. There isn't a film any more.

THE FRAU. *(closing her eyes, tight)* Cut!

THE BOY. *(a statement of fact, not vengeful)* There isn't a me any more.

THE FRAU. Get off of my set!

(Blackout.)

THE FRAU. Get off of my set

(Light returns, and the Frau is waking, with a start, in her armchair.)

THE FRAU. Get off of my

Chair.

(The Extra looking on from a distance. As the lights rise, we see that she is wearing somber period clothing for the first time.)

THE EXTRA. It is the middle of the night.

It is her own room.

Outside the window, the boots of the SS go

THE FRAU. *(whispered)* Left-right, left-right

THE EXTRA. Over the stones of the Preiser Platz.

Outside her window, she hears

THE FRAU. Glass breaking

THE EXTRA. All across the ancient part of the city.

The next day, the Frau builds a strong fire in the fireplace and feeds it her negatives. She does not look away, as the film is turned into strong black smoke that stays in her carpet and clothes for weeks. Everything you have seen goes up in flames.

Scene 25

Off Camera.

A LIST OF SCENES THAT NEVER MADE IT ON CAMERA.

(The Man and the Boy come out of the darkness to join the Extra. They too are wearing period clothing now.)

THE MAN. They give Achilles a triangle to wear, so they will know him when they see him.

THE BOY. Patroclus hides in a forest for twenty days.

THE EXTRA. The Amazon quits her sister and goes home to see their father die, filled with stones.

THE MAN. A child on the street points at Achilles and shouts.

THE BOY. Patroclus eats the bark off of trees.

THE EXTRA. The Amazon orders a thousand whiskeys in a thousand empty bars.

THE BOY. Patroclus dies of the cold, far from his own country.

THE MAN. Achilles boards a train to a place of no return.

THE EXTRA. The Amazon does nothing but watch.

THE MAN, THE BOY, THE EXTRA. Close up

Mid shot

Long shot

Out.

(Blackout.)

Epilogue

Off Camera.

(Light slowly returns. The Frau on her death bed many years later.)

THE FRAU. The Frau lived forever

THE EXTRA. As she'd always threatened to.

THE FRAU. She outlived the war. She outlived the century itself.

THE EXTRA. And year after year, the journalists asked her why she'd destroyed the film. On this, she always declined to comment

THE FRAU. Preferring to direct their attention to her fierce new hobby, hang-gliding.

THE EXTRA. She couldn't be pressed further, even with chocolate biscuits. And no one could have known that the negatives still looped through her dreams.

(Light rises on the Man and Boy around the bed, watching her.)

THE FRAU. When she finally died, the cameras came to see it

THE MAN. To catch a last glimpse of her

THE BOY. Before an everlasting life,
off camera.

THE EXTRA. And she found it impossible not to direct the cameramen from her death bed.

THE FRAU. *(out, as if to the cameramen)* Closer.

(During the following, the lights slowly dim to focus on the Frau, as if zooming to an extreme close-up.

As the lights dim, the Boy, the Man, and the Extra are edged out of the "frame", one by one.)

Bring the camera close, or you won't find anything.
I am not afraid to look like an old woman.

THE EXTRA. And a strange thing:

THE FRAU. Closer

THE BOY. The closer the cameras came...

(The Boy is outside of the frame now.)

THE FRAU. Closer

THE MAN. ...The less they saw of her.

(The Man is outside the frame now.)

THE FRAU. Closer

THE EXTRA. Until once again, the Frau was alone at the center of the frame.

(The Extra is outside the frame now.)

THE FRAU. Bring it close enough to see behind my eyes. How else will you learn anything?

THE EXTRA. And her sister looked on, quietly, an Extra in the final scene of her life.

THE FRAU. Closer.

Closer.

Closer.

(Light fades.)

End of Play

OTHER TITLES AVAILABLE FROM SAMUEL FRENCH

DORIS TO DARLENE
Jordan Harrison

Comedy / 4m, 2f / Unit Set

Doris to Darlene, A Cautionary Valentine: In the candy-colored 1960s, biracial schoolgirl Doris is molded into pop star Darlene by a whiz-kid record producer who culls a top-ten hit out of Richard Wagner's "Liebestod." Rewind to the candy-colored 1860s, where Wagner is writing the melody that will become Darlene's hit song. Fast-forward to the not-so-candy-colored present, where a teenager obsesses over Darlene's music – and his music teacher. Three dissonant decades merge into an unlikely harmony in this time-jumping pop fairy tale about the dreams and disasters behind one transcendent song.

"*Doris to Darlene: A Cautionary Valentine*, at Playwrights Horizons, is a quirky and enjoyable love letter to music and its seductive power to make us lose ourselves… Harrison's language is by turns so punchy, poetic and observant."
- NY Daily News

"Mr. Harrison's play has an affectionate, music-loving heart."
- New York Times

"Doris to Darlene has much going for it: Harrison's intelligence, originality and passion."
- Time Out New York

"Harrison's teasing, rapturous chamber opera of a play spins and crackles like a beloved old 78 under a bamboo needle... *Doris to Darlene* is that rare thing: a rarefied theatrical experiment that has the glow of pure entertainment and the warmth of a folktale."
- Newsday

SAMUELFRENCH.COM

OTHER TITLES AVAILABLE FROM SAMUEL FRENCH

EURYDICE
Sarah Ruhl

Dramatic Comedy / 5m, 2f / Unit Set

In *Eurydice*, Sarah Ruhl reimagines the classic myth of Orpheus through the eyes of its heroine. Dying too young on her wedding day, Eurydice must journey to the underworld, where she reunites with her father and struggles to remember her lost love. With contemporary characters, ingenious plot twists, and breathtaking visual effects, the play is a fresh look at a timeless love story.

"RHAPSODICALLY BEAUTIFUL. A weird and wonderful new play - an inexpressibly moving theatrical fable about love, loss and the pleasures and pains of memory."
- The New York Times

"EXHILARATING!! A luminous retelling of the Orpheus myth, lush and limpid as a dream where both author and audience swim in the magical, sometimes menacing, and always thrilling flow of the unconscious."
- *The New Yorker*

"Exquisitely staged by Les Waters and an inventive design team... Ruhl's wild flights of imagination, some deeply affecting passages and beautiful imagery provide transporting pleasures. They conspire to create original, at times breathtaking, stage pictures."
- *Variety*

"Touching, inventive, invigoratingly compact and luminously liquid in its rhythms and design, *Eurydice* reframes the ancient myth of ill-fated love to focus not on the bereaved musician but on his dead bride – and on her struggle with love beyond the grave as both wife and daughter."
- *The San Francisco Chronicle*

SAMUELFRENCH.COM